3.8 ~/
0.5 pt

Satan the Bull

Dave and Pat Sargent are longtime residents of Prairie Grove, Arkansas. Dave, a fourth-generation dairy farmer, began writing in early December 1990, and Pat, a former teacher, began writing shortly after. They enjoy the outdoors and have a real love for animals.

Satan the Bull

By

Dave and Pat Sargent

Illustrated by
Jeane Huff

Ozark Publishing, Inc.
P.O. Box 228
Prairie Grove, AR 72753

Library of Congress cataloging-in-publication data

Sargent, Dave, 1941—
    Satan the bull / by Dave and Pat Sargent ; illus-
trated by Jeane Huff.
    p. cm.
    Summary: Satan is such a mean bull that Farmer
John tries to sell him, but when he becomes a hero the
farmer has a change of heart.
    ISBN 1-56763-390-0 (cloth). — ISBN 1-56763-
391-9 (pbk)
    1.Bulls—Juvenile Fiction. [1. Bulls—Fiction.]
I. Sargent, Pat, 1936— .
    II. Huff, Jeane, 1946— ill. III. Title.
vPZ10.3.S243Sat 1998   97-29404
    [Fic]—dc21   CIP
                               AC

Printed in the United States of America

iv

Inspired by

a mean Jersey bull we had on our dairy farm.

Dedicated to

all children who have been chased by a bull. That kind of excitement we can do without!

Foreword

Satan was the meanest bull in northwest Arkansas, maybe the whole world. When Farmer John's two little girls venture into Satan's pasture, he quickly puts them out! One of the girls cuts her leg wide open crawling through the barbed-wire fence. This upsets Farmer John, and the next Sunday paper carries a want ad that reads:

For Sale: Jersey Bull $75.00

Satan redeems himself when an old gray timber wolf with rabies wanders onto Farmer John's place.

Contents

Satan the Bull

If you would like to have the authors of the Animal Pride Series visit your school, free of charge, call 1-800-321-5671 or 1-800-960-3876.

One

The Pitchfork

Ole Satan was the meanest bull in northwest Arkansas, in the whole world, maybe. He was not only mean, he was distrusting, too. He didn't trust anyone. But, then, Farmer John and his family didn't trust Satan, either, especially if their backs were turned.

Satan was a big Jersey bull who demanded, and got, respect from anyone who dared enter his pasture. He had put many a full-grown man on the run. He was chocolate-brown in color, except for his shoulders and part of his face. That part was black. He was a real handsome bull, but boy, he was mean! Yep! That Satan was one mean bull!

Everyone on Farmer John's place was upset with ole Satan. They were upset because he had chased two of Farmer John's little girls out of his pasture, and one of the girls had cut her leg real bad.

Actually, no one could really blame Satan for chasing the girls, because the girls knew they should not be in his pasture. When they were scrambling under the fence, trying to escape Satan'sw rath, Amber, the older one, ripped her leg wide open on the barbed wire.

That's why everyone was upset with ole Satan. They kept asking, "Why does Satan have to be so mean? Why does he have to have such a bad disposition? Why can't he be like the cows? They're gentle. Satan can't get along with anyone!

He doesn't even try! And that ole bull is so distrusting! Look into his eyes. Ole Satan doesn't trust anyone!"

Farmer John had always made sure that he was the one who fed Satan. He would not allow Molly or his girls, Amber, April, and Ashley, to feed Satan. Farmer John, himself, wouldn't turn his back on the bull. He kept an eye out for ole Satan every minute he was in his pasture.

The day after Amber ripped her leg open trying to get away from Satan, Farmer John wondered if he should sell the bull. Maybe that's what he should do. Maybe he should just up and sell that bull. After all, Farmer John's place should be a safe place to raise his three little girls. Who knows, if Amber hadn't been a fast runner, Satan might have killed her. No doubt about it, ole Satan was mean! And because he was so mean, he might have to go.

That night while Farmer John was putting the cows into the corral, getting ready to start the milking, Satan slipped in with them. Now, Farmer John had his head turned in the other direction and didn't see ole Satan come in.

With only three cows left to be milked, Fanny decided she would skip milking, even though it was her turn. She went to the back gate and, sticking her long neck through the small opening, lifted the latch. The gate swung open, and she calmly walked out just as Farmer John looked out the back door.

"You come back here, Fanny!"
Farmer John yelled. "You know it's
your turn! You get back in here,
right now!" Well, Fanny just kept
on walking. She walked right up to
the fresh hay that Farmer John had
put out.

The cows always came in to be milked in a certain order. Once in a while one of them missed a turn, but not very often.

"Fanny has never missed her turn before. Something must be bothering that cow," Farmer John reasoned.

About that time, something hard, bumpy, and sharp caught him under the seat of his pants and lifted him up into the air.

Just as Farmer John came down, much to his surprise, the same thing happened again! This time, he sailed up and over the fence and landed on the ground outside the corral. He landed smack on his back with a thud! "Tarnation!" he yelled at the top of his lungs. "What in the cat hair was that?"

Farmer John added, "If I didn't know better, I'd think that mean ole Satan was in . . ." Farmer John's voice trailed off as he spotted Satan pawing the ground inside the corral.

"You dad-blamed ole bull! What are you doing in the corral?" Farmer John yelled. "You're not supposed to be in there! You're the one that caused all the trouble with Fanny. That's why she took off!"

Whirling, Farmer John headed for the covered pen at the side of the barn where he doctored sick cows. That's where he kept his pitchfork. He grabbed the pitchfork and ran to the corral. There stood ole Satan, as peaceful as a lamb.

The actions of his dad were going through Farmer John's head. His daddy always took a pitchfork to a bull as soon as it was full grown. He would work the bull over good with a pitchfork, jab it time after time, just to show that bull who was boss! His dad never ever had a problem

with the bull after that. Farmer John
drew back his hand, the pitchfork
gleaming in the last rays of sun.

With a quick jab, his arm came forward. Farmer John shook his head as the fork stuck in the ground. He couldn't do it. He remembered he had always felt sorry for the bull.

Farmer John opened the back gate and ole Satan ambled out. He headed for his pasture, not once looking back. That's when the thought hit Farmer John. He would sell the dad-blamed bull!

TWO

Jersey Bull for Sale

Farmer John placed an ad in the Sunday paper. It read:

FOR SALE
JERSEY BULL $75.00
Farmer John's Place. See John.

Farmer John, Molly, and the girls were sitting on the back porch that afternoon eating big bowls of homemade strawberry ice cream.

After Farmer John finished his bowl, he picked up the paper, turned to the FOR SALE section, and read aloud, "Rip-snortin', fire-eatin' Jersey Bull for sale. $75,000.00! Goes by the name of Satan."

"Daddy!" the girls exclaimed. "Satan's not a fire-eating bull!"

Amber jumped up and looked over Farmer John's shoulder. "That doesn't say $75,000.00, Daddy!"

By that time, April had moved over beside her daddy. She said, "Daddy! Can't you read? The ad says: For sale: Jersey bull $75.00."

Farmer John chuckled. He loved to tease the three little girls. He figured the ad would bring him a "taker" first thing Monday morning.

Well, Farmer John was wrong. There were no "takers" Monday, Tuesday, or Wednesday.

"Humph!" Farmer John said, as he prepared for bed on Wednesday night. "I was certain someone would snap up ole Satan tonight after prayer meeting was over, but no one even mentioned his name. What do you think, Molly? You reckon no one reads the Sunday paper?"

Molly smiled. She said, "John, I think everyone read your ad. I also think that everyone knows how mean Satan is. I'm sure they have all heard about Satan and about Amber's cut leg. You know how stories get added to and changed. By now, they may be saying that Satan gored her, that his long, curved horns ripped her leg open!"

Farmer John's eyes widened a little. "Dad blame, Molly! You reckon that's why no one's stopped by to haggle over the price?"

Molly smiled. "Could be, John. It could be."

For the next Sunday edition, Farmer John had the ad amended to read:

FOR SALE
GOOD JERSEY BULL $50.00

You guessed it. No "takers."
The third Sunday, the AD read:

FOR SALE
JERSEY BULL $25.00

When no one responded to the low price of $25.00, Farmer John knew for sure that everyone thought Satan was just too mean to have around. Yep! They were right. Satan was one mean bull!

Three

The Rabid Wolf

Early the next morning, when Barney and Farmer John were bringing in the cows, things went crazy. Cows began bawling, baby calves began crying, and every animal on the place sounded an alarm.

Farmer John stopped, listened, then went into action. "I'm going back for my gun," he said, as he ran for the back door. "You go ahead, Barney; see what's wrong."

Loading his gun as he ran, Farmer John now realized that most of the commotion was coming from Satan's pasture. He emerged from the trees just as something flew through the air and landed with a thud. Satan was on it by the time it hit the ground! He gored it with his horns again and again.

Farmer John squinted his eyes. His heart almost stopped. Satan was killing ole Barney. No! He threw up his double-barreled shotgun, his finger squeezing both triggers.

"I'm gonna kill that dad-blamed bull, once and for all!" He would have, too, but a familiar whine stopped him. Something brushed against his leg. He looked down. There stood Barney. "Then who . . . ?" He stopped, confused.

Satan gored the animal one
more time and, with his horns still in
it, turned and twisted and pushed
hard against the ground.

Satan held the animal down for a long time, then slowly raised his bloody head. He stared at the still form on the ground, then bellering, began backing away. He went down on his knees and wiped his mouth, his face, and his neck on the grass.

Farmer John and Barney stood watching. Then, suddenly, Farmer John realized what every animal, including Barney, already knew. That animal lying dead was rabid. "That's it! Right? It has rabies!"

Farmer John climbed through the fence and eased over toward the dead animal. When Satan saw Farmer John in his pasture, he began slowly backing away, his head low to the ground. He didn't want any trouble with Farmer John. Satan remembered him standing with a pitchfork in his hand.

Farmer John leaned down. "Yep, it's dead, all right. It's a wolf. I've never seen it around here before. This wolf had rabies, for sure." And looking at Satan, he figured Satan would be next. He started walking

toward Satan, but Satan backed
away.

"Come on, Satan. Let me look you over good. If you've got a cut or a scrape on you from this wolf, I'm gonna have to kill you, boy. Can't have you infecting the cows and calves or anything else that runs through your field. Come on now, be still." Farmer John's voice was calm, but Satan kept backing away. He turned and walked across the field, heading for the trees where he liked to lie.

The school bell rang across the land, and everyone rushed to the school. The news of a rabid wolf showing up on Farmer John's place terrified everyone. The wolf had infected everyone and every animal it had laid a tooth on.

Every child was checked for bite marks, and every animal was checked, too. When everyone met back at the school the very next day, they agreed that a miracle had saved them all. That miracle was Satan, the Jersey bull. Several men tried to buy Satan that day; that is, *if* he had not been bitten by the rabid wolf. But Farmer John smiled and shook his head, saying, "No, thanks, boys. I've decided to keep him."

Well, it clouded up and rained hard while Farmer John was doing the morning milking. He got a good look at ole Satan later in the day. There were no bite marks on him, no broken skin anywhere. It looked like Satan would be saved. But Farmer John moved Satan to a small, more secure pen, where he could keep an eye on him, night and day.

When enough time had passed, Satan was still healthy, and it was proclaimed to the entire county. The rabies scare was over.

Satan had saved the day, so to speak. He had killed the rabid wolf before the wolf did any damage to Farmer John's place or to any other. And everyone was grateful to Satan. That did it. Satan's life was spared.

And Farmer John didn't run any more ads in the Sunday paper. The incident didn't exactly change ole Satan's disposition. He was still mean and distrusting, but at least he had learned something important. He realized now that Farmer John must like him just a little. And maybe he did try to be a little nicer. He stopped chasing the wild animals when they cut across his pasture.

Yep! Satan remained Satan. Ole Satan was one mean bull!

Four

Jersey Bull Facts

The Jersey bull is a smaller bull than most dairy breeds. Their small horns curve inward. They weigh from eight hundred to one thousand pounds.

Jersey cattle came from the tiny British island of Jersey in the English Channel. They were brought to the United States in 1850.

Jersey cattle range in color from gray to dark fawn, or reddish-brown. Some are a dark chocolate-brown and appear almost black.

Jerseys are rugged animals. They can do well in rough country. Farmers, often in isolated areas, select cattle that are best adapted to their particular environments and that yield the products in greatest demand. In the United States, Jersey cows are raised mostly for their milk. Jersey bulls are used for breeding purposes.